To Saskia, Camille, Keiko, and James

The Missing Pairs
Copyright © 2021 by Yvonne Ivinson
All rights reserved. Manufactured in Italy. For information address HarperCollins Children's Books,
a division of HarperCollins Publishers, 195 Broadway, New York, NY 10007. www.harpercollinschildrens.com

Acrylic paint was used to prepare the full-color art. The text type is Century Gothic.

Library of Congress Cataloging-in-Publication Data

Names: Ivinson, Yvonne, author, illustrator. Title: The missing pairs / Yvonne Ivinson.
Description: First edition. | New York : Greenwillow Books, an imprint of HarperCollinsPublishers, [2021] | Audience: Ages 4-8. |
    Audience: Grades K-1. | Summary: Illustrations and easy-to-read text follow Bear as he tries to help Fox, Hare, and Badger find
    one missing sock, one missing mitten, and one missing boot.
Identifiers: LCCN 2020053832 | ISBN 9780062842893 (hardcover)
Subjects: CYAC: Lost and found possessions—Fiction. | Animals—Fiction. | Humorous stories.
Classification: LCC PZ7.1.I9845 Mis 2021 | DDC [E]—dc23 LC record available at https://lccn.loc.gov/2020053832

21 22 23 24 25 RTLO 10 9 8 7 6 5 4 3 2 1 First Edition   Greenwillow Books

YVONNE IVINSON

THE MISSING PAIRS

LOST

Call Fox

GREENWILLOW BOOKS. *An Imprint of* HarperCollins*Publishers*

"**W**hat's up, Fox?" said Bear.

"I've lost my sock," said Fox.
"Look, I have one bare paw."
"Are you cold?" asked Bear.

"My toes are cold," said Fox.

"I need two socks. I need a pair."

"Oh, I know where to go,"
said Bear. "I'll tow you."

"Hello there," said Fox to Hare.

"I've lost a sock and I need a pair.

Do you have a spare?"

"No, Fox," said Hare.
"And look! I've lost my mitten
and have one bare paw.
I need a pair, too."

"Jump in my box, Hare,"
said Fox. "Bear knows
where to go."

"Hello, Badger," said Fox. "We're missing our sock and mitten pairs."
"Do you have any spares?" asked Hare.

"No. And look!" said Badger.
"I've lost my boot and have one
bare foot. I need a pair, too."

"Hop in my box, Badger," said Fox.
"Bear knows where to go."

"Almost there," said Bear.

"No, no, no! NO!
Not pear, Bear. PAIR!"

"Not pear?" asked Bear.

"Now we'll never find them,"
said Fox. "And I love my socks."

"I love my mittens," said Hare.

"I love my boots," said Badger.

"I love pears," said Bear.

"Wait, are those our missing pairs?"